LARK
STEALS THE SHOW

NATASHA DEEN
Illustrated by MARCUS CUTLER

orca Echoes

ORCA BOOK PUBLISHERS

Published in Canada and the United States in 2022 by Orca Book Publishers.
orcabook.com

Library and Archives Canada Cataloguing in Publication
Title: Lark steals the show / Natasha Deen ; illustrated by Marcus Cutler.
Other titles: Steals the show
Names: Deen, Natasha, author. | Cutler, Marcus, 1978- illustrator.
Series: Orca echoes.
Description: Series statement: Orca echoes
Identifiers: Canadiana (print) 20210349131 | Canadiana (ebook) 2021034914X |
ISBN 9781459831575 (softcover) | ISBN 9781459831582 (PDF) | ISBN 9781459831599 (EPUB)
Classification: LCC PS8607.E444 L38 2022 | DDC jC813/.6—dc23

Library of Congress Control Number: 2021948821

Summary: In this illustrated early chapter book, Lark and Connor are called upon to defend
their friend when he is framed in the theft of a fellow student's artwork at an art show.

Orca Book Publishers is committed to reducing the consumption of
nonrenewable resources in the production of our books. We make
every effort to use materials that support a sustainable future.

Orca Book Publishers gratefully acknowledges the support for its publishing
programs provided by the following agencies: the Government of Canada,
the Canada Council for the Arts and the Province of British Columbia
through the BC Arts Council and the Book Publishing Tax Credit.

Cover artwork and interior illustrations by Marcus Cutler
Author photo by Curtis Comeau

Printed and bound in Canada.

25 24 23 22 • 1 2 3 4

Chapter One

My name is Lark Ba, and I'm about to miss the boat. Not really. I'm in my bedroom, and it's on dry land. Missing the boat is something my halmoni—that's Korean for *grandmother*—says when I'm running late.

I am behind Halmoni's ~~skedule~~ ~~schkedjool~~ schedule because I want to look really nice. Halmoni is taking me and Connor—he's my little brother—to the art gallery. There is a big show today, and our friend Franklin is one of the artists. His paintings are dynamite!

"Lark!" Connor knocked on my bedroom door.

I opened my door and twirled. I wore blue leggings and a gray sweater with calculators on it. "Ready! You look nice too."

Connor grinned. "Thanks, Lark!"

Aren't I such a great big sister?

"I'm wearing my trench coat in case we run into a mystery," he said and twirled too.

This summer had been the bestest! Connor and I had become private investigators. We'd helped Mrs. Robinson find the lost key to the library and found out who had stolen a pair of diamond earrings from the general store. Connor and I are really very good detectives.

"Being prepared for a case is a great idea," I told Connor.

His grin got bigger.

Aren't I the bestest big sister? "I'm going to get my fedora. A detective needs to wear a cool hat!"

"Kids!" Halmoni called from the kitchen. "Hurry!"

We ran downstairs. Dad and Halmoni had made chocolate-zucchini muffins, which smelled delicious! I mixed a dish of food for Max, our dog. Then I had a muffin. It was so yummy, I had two more.

"Are you and Mom going to come to the art gallery too?" I asked Dad.

He nodded. "And we are bringing a big surprise for you!"

"Cool!" said Connor.

"You know," Halmoni said, tapping her chin, "Babu might like to hear about the art show."

Babu—that's Swahili for *grandfather*—is Mom's dad. Halmoni is Dad's mom.

"That's a great idea," said Dad. "Shall we call him?"

Connor and I nodded because our mouths were too full of yummy muffins to talk.

Babu was in Kenya, counting elephants. He grinned when he saw everyone on-screen. "What a nice surprise!" He held up a photo of a baby elephant. "Look, Eliza had her calf. Isn't she beautiful? We were just discussing what to name her."

"I know!" said Connor. "Halley, like the comet. Lark and I are reading all about it in our astronomy books."

I nodded. "Every seventy-five years, it comes close to Earth. You can see it without a telescope."

"Halley," said Babu. "I like it! I'll take it to the team."

Dad said goodbye and left for work as we told Babu about the art show.

"The theme is fruits and vegetables. Today the final artwork is going to be on display," said Connor.

"Wow," said Babu, "that sounds amazing. I wish I could be there."

"Me too," I said. "We miss you."

We finished talking to Babu, and then we cleaned up our snack. Just as we were putting our dishes away, there was a knock at the door.

"I wonder who that might be," said Halmoni.

"Do you think it might be someone who needs Connor and me to solve a mystery?" I asked.

"There's only one way to find out," she said.

Connor and I followed her to the door.

Chapter Two

The person on the other side of the door was Sophie McCallister. She's my best friend, and for the longest time she didn't even know it! But guess what? She helped us with a couple of our cases, and I think she knows we're besties now!

"Sophie Sofa," said Connor.

She grinned. "Hello, Connor Wool and Baa Baa Lark Sheep."

I grinned back. Our last name is Ba, and *baa* is the sound sheep make. I like the nickname, but Connor doesn't. Instead Sophie decided to call him Connor Wool because wool is warm and cozy. He calls her Sophie Sofa because the two words sound alike. It's nice for us to have nicknames for each other. "What are you doing here?"

"I have a gift for you, Connor and Max," said Sophie. She reached into her backpack and pulled out three shirts with alligators on them.

"Oh, wow!" gasped Connor. "So cool! Thank you!"

"My babushka helped me make them. It's my way of saying thanks for helping me all those times I needed help," she said. "I remembered that alligators are your favorite, Lark."

"They are!" I said. "And they rhyme with *investigators*, which I love!"

Connor helped Max into his shirt. "We're going to the gallery because Franklin is in the art show," he said. "It's going to start in an hour, but he said we can come early and hang out. Do you want to come with us?"

"That would be fun," said Sophie. "Let me call and ask my mom." After she got ~~permisshun~~ ~~premisstion~~ permission, we followed Halmoni outside.

It was a bright, sunny day, and the air smelled like wind and flowers. Max sniffed everything as we walked.

"What do you think Franklin's painting will be?" I asked.

"When we were at the library, he borrowed a bunch of books on fruit trees." Connor's face went frowny. "We were having lots of fun until Kyle showed up."

"Ugh, Kyle," said Sophie. "He's the meanest kid in our whole school, but he's especially mean to Franklin."

Halmoni gently tugged Max away from a fire hydrant. "Is Kyle always mean to Franklin?"

"Always," we said in unison.

"The teachers have tried everything to get Kyle to be nicer," Sophie said. "They've had Franklin and Kyle work together on class projects, and they brought in their parents." She shrugged. "It doesn't change anything. When Kyle gets in trouble for being mean, he apologizes, but then he just does it again."

"Hmm," said Halmoni. "I don't like the sound of that."

"No one likes it," said Sophie. "Especially Franklin. He tries hard to be Kyle's friend, but it never works out."

"Then let's make sure Franklin feels very special today," said Halmoni.

Soon we were at the gallery. It was pyramid-shaped and made of glass, and it had four exhibition rooms, A, B, C and D. In the sunshine it sparkled and shone.

Connor ran up to the building. He pressed his hands against the glass and peered inside.

The reflections of Sophie and me bounced as we ran and pressed our hands against the glass. We could see the artists inside. Mr. and Mrs. Lee from the general store were there. And Mrs. Robinson, the librarian, was beside them!

"There's Franklin! Kate is with him!" Connor said.

Sophie and I looked. They sat next to our friend Loi. She was beside Miss Ruby and Mr. Rupert.

Franklin saw us. He waved.

"Max and I are going to finish our walk," Halmoni said to us. "Your parents and I will meet you in a bit, inside the gallery. We'll be there with bells on!"

We hugged her goodbye.

"Won't bells make a lot of noise?" asked Connor after she had left.

I nodded. "When they get here, let's make sure they put the bells away."

"Agreed," said Connor. "We don't want them to get in trouble."

As we walked inside, we saw Monty, the security guard. "Hello, Lark and Connor," he said.

"Hello," I said. "We're here for the show!"

"Have fun!" Monty said. "Be careful not to touch any of the artwork, okay?" He waved goodbye and walked away.

Around us, there were families with kids, families without kids, groups of friends and people by themselves. They were exploring the other exhibits as they waited for the art show to start.

Franklin and Kate met us at the main doors.

"You came!" said Franklin. "This is so exciting!" He did a little jig. "Did you know that at the end of the show Mx. Tradewell is putting everyone's name in a jar? They're going to pull out ten names, and those artists will have their work in the gallery for a whole month! And someone might actually buy it!"

Connor hugged him. "I hope you get picked!"

"Franklin did a painting with of all of us in it," said Kate. She giggled. "You're going to love it!"

Suddenly Kyle appeared from Exhibit Room A. "I heard you talking about Franklin's art," he said. "I don't know why you want to see it. It's not that great."

"Did you see it?" Sophie demanded.

"I don't have to see it," said Kyle. "If you want to see something amazing, you should look at my painting."

"Franklin is amazing too," said Sophie. She glared at him. "He's so amazing that he always beats you in class."

Kyle glowered. "Not always! Come look at my art. It's better than Franklin's."

"He was good enough to be part of today's event," I said. I was trying not to use my grumpy voice, but it was hard. Kyle was being ruder than usual!

"I'd love to see your work," Franklin said to Kyle. "I bet it's really awesome." He looked at the clock on the wall. "There's about an hour before the show starts. Do you want to show us your piece and tell us about it?"

Kyle's chest puffed out. "Follow me." He strode to Exhibit Room A.

Franklin followed. The rest of us didn't move.

"Come on, guys," said Franklin. "Let's go."

"Why?" asked Kate. "He's never nice to any of us. And he's really mean to you. He shouldn't have said any of those things."

"I agree," said Franklin, "but maybe if we're kind, he'll see he doesn't have to be mean."

Franklin, Kate and Sophie walked over to Kyle's exhibit.

Connor and I hung back.

"I don't like this," said Connor. "Kyle always picks fights with Franklin."

"I have a squiggly feeling in my tummy too," I said.

"Do you think Kyle would do something to Franklin's work?" asked Connor.

"You mean like..." I tried to think of the word. It was a good one, and it started with a *c* or an *s*, and it meant to be sneaky and destroy people's stuff.

"We should look out for Franklin," said Connor.

Before I could say anything, we heard shouting.

Connor and I raced toward the noise. I didn't like what I saw, not one little bit. Nope, nope, nope.

Chapter Three

Sophie stood between Franklin and Kyle.

"You're trying to destroy my work!" shouted Kyle. "You know you're not supposed to touch a canvas."

Franklin lifted up his hands. "I didn't touch anything, I promise." He spoke softly. "I was just looking at the shade of red on your painting. It's cadmium red, right?"

"Don't touch my things!" Kyle yelled.

Connor and I looked at Kyle's painting. It was a watercolor of a bowl of red apples in a lime-green bowl on a table. There was also a black kitten sleeping next to a pie.

"It's good," whispered Connor. "I was hoping it wouldn't be nice."

I thought about what Franklin had said. "You should tell Kyle. Maybe it will stop him from being so mean."

Connor made a face.

"I like your painting," I told Kyle. Then I thought of a ~~spefic~~ ~~speciphic~~ specific compliment I could give. "The apples are very realistic."

Kyle squinted at me. "Of course they are," he said.

Connor nodded. "I like the kitten. They look full of mischief." He nudged Sophie.

"Oh, hmm," said Sophie. "My babushka and I love to bake. Your pie looks like I could pick it up and eat it."

Kyle didn't say anything.

Sophie glared at him. "You could at least say thanks when we say nice things."

"True artists don't care about compliments," said Kyle. "You'd understand if you were a real artist, like me."

Sophie's cheeks went as red as Kyle's apples.

"Let's go look at Franklin's painting," I said hastily. I grabbed hold of Sophie's hand and pulled her away.

"Oh, Franklin!" I laughed and clapped my hands. "I love your painting!" Franklin had painted himself as a bunch of grapes. On the canvas his grape self was painting us. Connor was an orange, I was an apple, Sophie was a lime, and Kate was a banana.

"I love it," said Kate.

"Look at this." Franklin lifted the painting off the easel and took it to the window. "I used glitter." He tilted it from side to side. The bright sunshine made it sparkle. "See? It makes it shiny."

We cheered, and Franklin blushed with pleasure.

Just then Mx. Tradewell came into the hall.

I really liked them! Mx. Tradewell had long, curly blond hair and brown eyes. They were wearing a black shirt that had images of paintbrushes with paint dripping off their ends. They waved at us, then turned to face the people in the hall. "Artists, you've been busy setting up! If you'd like to take a break, there are snacks in the cafeteria."

Some artists moved to the exit. Some continued setting up.

"Do you want me to show you the art in Exhibit Hall B?" asked Franklin. "It's an exhibit on pointillism."

"Point-until-what-ism?" Sophie's face scrunched up.

Franklin laughed. "Pointillism. It's when an artist paints using dots."

"Wow," said Connor. "That sounds like hard work."

"It is, but it's supercool to see up close." Franklin put his canvas back on the easel. "I'll grab my stuff from the locker room and meet you there."

"I can show you guys where it is," said Kate, and she led the way to the hall.

We stopped in front of the first painting. Franklin was right about how cool these paintings were.

"Man," said Connor. "I bet it takes a lot of patience to do something like that."

The sudden pounding of footsteps made us turn around.

Kyle rushed into the hall. His face was red and he was breathing hard. "Did you see him?"

"See who?" I asked.

"Franklin." He bent over to catch his breath. "I was going to the cafeteria when I saw Franklin go back to Exhibit Hall A," said Kyle. "By the time I got there, Franklin was gone, and so was my painting! He stole my painting!"

"Franklin's not a thief!" Sophie stepped close to Kyle.

Just then Franklin came into the hall. His backpack was on his shoulder, and Mx. Tradewell was with him.

"What did you do with my painting?" Kyle yelled at him.

Franklin blinked in surprise. "Your painting? Nothing."

"I know you took it. Give it back," said Kyle.

"But I don't have it," said Franklin.

Mx. Tradewell put their hand on Kyle's shoulder to calm him down. "Why don't we take a look together? Maybe someone moved it by mistake."

"I wouldn't take your artwork," Franklin said to Kyle.

Kyle didn't say anything.

Mx. Tradewell gave Franklin a sympathetic smile.

"We know you wouldn't," said Sophie. "Forget about Kyle, and tell us why you like these paintings."

Franklin reached into his bag. "I have this great book on the history of pointillism." He pulled out the book, and a rolled piece of canvas fell out of the backpack and dropped to the floor.

"That's my painting!" Kyle glared at Franklin. "I knew you'd stolen my painting!"

Franklin looked like he wanted to cry. "But I didn't do it," he said miserably. "I didn't put that in my bag."

And just like that, my best day became my worst day.

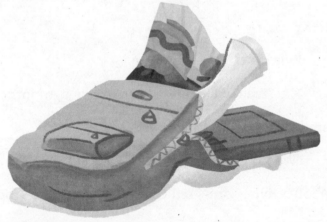

Chapter Four

"Oh, Franklin," said Mx. Tradewell, picking up the canvas. "This *is* Kyle's artwork."

Franklin blinked back tears. "But I didn't take it." He gestured to the painting. "And I would never cut a canvas from its frame."

I concentrated. There was a mystery to solve. "This is easy to figure out," I said. In my favorite detective novels, the P.I. asks about security cameras, so I said, "The gallery has cameras. We can look at the videos."

Mx. Tradewell shook their head. "We've been having trouble with the cameras. Monty said the repair guys will be in next week."

"This doesn't makes sense," Connor said. "If Franklin had done this horrible thing, why would he put the evidence in his bag?"

Kyle pushed in front of us. "He did it because he was jealous."

Mx. Tradewell faced Franklin. "Can you prove you *didn't* do this?"

Franklin shook his head.

"But you were in the room recently, right?" Mx. Tradewell knelt next to him. "Did you see anyone or hear anything?"

Again Franklin shook his head. "Loi was leaving as I came in. But I was by myself. I went to the bathroom, and then I came here."

"Franklin didn't do this!" Kate burst out. "He wouldn't!" She stomped over to Kyle.

He ducked behind Mx. Tradewell.

"Lark and Connor," said the gallery owner. "You helped find the person who was playing pranks at the community theater, and you helped discover who was sabotaging the baking contest. Will you help me find out what happened here?"

"We can promise to try our hardest to do it," I said.

Mx. Tradewell nodded. "That's good enough for me," they said.

"No one's supposed to touch other artists' work. Everyone knows that!" Kyle sniffed and blinked away his tears. "This was my big chance to prove to everyone what a great artist I am. Now it's gone!" He ran to the exit.

"I'm going to make sure he's all right," said Mx. Tradewell. They turned to Franklin, and their face was frowny. "Franklin, you understand that if Lark and Connor can't prove you didn't do this, I'll have to exclude you from the show."

Franklin nodded. Then he began to cry.

Connor and I put our arms around him.

"We're going to work really hard to solve this case," I said. "We have almost an hour, and there's two of us—"

"Three of us," Sophie interrupted. "I'm going to help."

"Me too," said Kate. "No one gets to lie about my friend and get away with it."

Franklin smiled through his tears. "I'm lucky to have friends like you."

I tried to smile, but my insides were growling. Kate was right. No one should get away with lying about someone else. I promised myself that we would clear Franklin's name. And I knew just how to start.

Chapter Five

"We need to talk to everyone," I said, "Monty, the other people who work here, the artists and the visitors."

Connor's face went squiggly. "There are a lot of people. That's going to be a lot of talking."

"That's good news," I said. "With all these people, someone must have seen something, right?"

Connor straightened and smiled. "Right," he said.

"What about delivery people?" asked Sophie. "Maybe one of them saw someone doing something."

These were all great ideas. We split into two groups. Connor and I would talk to Monty and the gallery ~~employeeze~~ ~~emploiese~~ employees. Sophie, Franklin and Kate would talk to the artists.

Connor patted his pockets. "Does anyone have paper and a pencil? We should write down what people say."

Franklin smiled. "An artist always has paper and pencils." He reached into his bag and handed them out. Then we split up.

"Do you want me to take our notes?" Connor asked.

I have dyslexia, which means I mix up letters and numbers. It also means I have to be patient with myself when it comes to printing. Usually I take the notes, but today we had to hurry if we were going to help Franklin. "You do it," I said. "You're faster."

Connor put the paper and pencil in his pocket.

"We need to solve this before people believe Franklin did it," I said.

Connor thought. "The painting must have been stolen when everyone left for snacks."

"You're right," I said. "Let's start at the scene of the crime."

"Great idea," said Connor.

"Aren't I a supersmart big sister?" I asked as we headed to the main hall.

Connor sighed. "Twins, Lark. We're twins."

"But I'm older!"

"By ten minutes," said Connor.

"That counts," I insisted. "I'm older."

Connor stopped. "Okay, you're older." He grinned. "But I'm smarter."

"What? You are not!"

"And better looking," he said as he went into Exhibit Hall A.

"You are not!" I argued.

"And taller," he said. "I'm much, much taller!"

"Only by two inches!" Ugh. Little brothers can be so annoying.

"This one must be Kyle's," I said. It was the only easel without a painting on it. I crouched down and checked the floor for footprints. Zilch. So much for being able to follow them back to the culprit.

"Hmm, there's a small smudge of paint," Connor said, pointing at the easel. "It's green." He wrote that down.

I inspected the smudge. "And it's still wet."

"Lark, Connor." Mx. Tradewell came into the room. "How are you doing?"

"Good," said Connor. "We're looking around the easel to see if there are any clues."

"Do you see anything?" they asked.

"Wet paint," said Connor.

That tickled my brain. It made me think of the canvas in Franklin's bag, but I couldn't put the clues together. That made me feel grumpy, because we didn't have a lot of time.

"A penny for your thoughts," Mx. Tradewell said to me.

It didn't seem right for them to pay me for my thoughts, so I said, "I'll share them for free."

They laughed.

I didn't get the joke, but I didn't want them to feel bad, so I laughed too. Then I said, "The wet paint on the easel. It feels like a clue."

"Ah," said Mx. Tradewell. "It might be." They turned to the exit as someone called their name. "Good luck. Come and get me if I can help."

Connor watched them leave. His face was all frowny and confused. "Why did they laugh when you gave your thoughts for free?" He looked down at his feet.

"I don't know," I said, "but that mystery will have to wait. We better solve—oh! Wet paint!"

"Yeah," said Connor. "Wet paint! Right! If we can see which paintings aren't dry—"

"Maybe those artists were touching up their paintings when the culprit took Kyle's canvas. Maybe they saw something."

"Or maybe they were the ones who took it," Connor said grimly.

We walked around slow-like, looking at all the easels. Sometimes I had to crouch to see if a painting was wet. Sometimes Connor had to lean to the side to check.

"Anyone could have come and gone," Connor said as an artist came into the room. "And with people walking in and out of the room—"

"They could have carried away a clue without knowing," I said. Connor and I ran to the artist and asked if they had seen anything. The artist shook their head. We thanked them, then kept looking, but all the paintings were dry.

"How did green paint get on the easel but nowhere else?" Connor asked.

I wondered that too. Then the answer came to me. "Crickets!" I said. "What if it's like in our detective books when the bad guy wants to confuse the detective? The bad guy leaves a trail of false clues."

Connor snapped his fingers. "They call it a red herring!" He gave me a worried look. "If our bad guy is leaving red herrings, then how do we know which clues are real?"

"We're excellent private investigators," I said. "We'll figure it out." I smiled big so he wouldn't know I was worried about that too. "Come on. Let's see if Monty saw anything."

We found the security guard outside, watering some potted plants and checking their soil.

"Hello, kids." He dusted the dirt off his gardening gloves and smiled at us. "What's up?"

We told him what had happened.

His face went white, then pink. "Oh no!" He glanced at the pots. "I was in the main hall earlier, and I saw Ms. Jensen, the gardener, outside. She saw me too and waved." He gestured to the watering hose. "And accidentally sprayed herself with water. So I came out to help while she changed." He paced one way, then the other. "This is terrible! And our cameras aren't even working in the main hall. I have to go and see if I can help Mx. Tradewell!" He rushed inside.

"Wait!" called Connor. "We have questions!"

"Maybe it's better if we ask him later," I said. "He seemed really upset."

"Yeah, I guess I'd be too," said Connor, "if I was a security guard and someone stole a painting on my watch."

"Let's see if Kate, Franklin and Sophie had any luck," I said.

We went to the cafeteria. Miss Ruby and Mr. Rupert were there, sharing a slice of pie.

"Hello, Lark and Connor," said Miss Ruby. "Would you like to sit with us?"

Connor explained why we were there.

Mr. Rupert's face went all sad. "It's horrible that someone would steal Kyle's painting. It was very good."

"It's terrible that Franklin's been accused," said Miss Ruby. "He'd never do anything like that!"

Then she smiled. "But with the two of you on the case, I know you'll find out who's responsible for it."

Mr. Rupert nodded. "That's right! After all, you found our missing pets at the fair, and that wasn't easy."

"Did you see anything when you were tidying up before the break?" asked Connor.

"I'm sorry," said Mr. Rupert. "We were the first people to leave."

"We're getting our snack, then taking our pets for a quick walk before the show begins," said Miss Ruby.

This was disappointing. I'd hoped for some clues or leads. But I remembered what one of the detectives from my book had said, so I said it too. "Thank you. If you remember anything, no matter how big or small, let us know."

"Wait," said Miss Ruby as we started to walk away. "You should check with Loi. She said she wanted to work a little longer before her break."

Excellent! "Thank you," I said.

Then Connor and I dashed off to find Loi.

Chapter Six

Loi was outside the main doors. She was eating a banana.

"Lark! Connor!" She put her banana peel in the compost bin. "How are you?"

"Not good," said Connor. "We came to cheer on Franklin, but something terrible has happened. Kyle's painting was found in Franklin's bag, and he's been accused of stealing it."

Loi gasped. "That's terrible! Franklin wouldn't do that!"

"Exactly! Miss Ruby said you stayed behind," I said. "Did you see anything?"

"That's true," said Loi. "I was the last one to leave the gallery. But I was so focused on getting everything ready." She tilted her head. "People were coming in and out all the time. I didn't pay attention to anyone until I heard Franklin call my name. He came over and we talked for a bit." She looked sadly at us. "When I left, he was the only person in the main hall."

"But was he the *last* person you saw coming in?" Connor asked as he wrote down what she'd said. "You didn't see anyone heading toward the main hall?"

"No one," she said miserably. Then she went still. "Although..."

Connor and I leaned forward.

"Just as I was leaving, we heard a noise in the back storage room. It was like...scuttling. We thought it was a mouse or something small. I was going to tell Monty or Mx. Tradewell after I finished my banana."

Hmm, I thought about investigating the storage room. Then I thought harder. A mouse wouldn't steal a painting, and Loi said the noise seemed to be from something small.

"Did anything else happen? Did you see or hear anything else?"

She shook her head. "I was really hungry, so I ran out."

"How long ago was that?" Connor asked.

She thought for a second. "Maybe twenty minutes ago?"

"Would that be long enough for Franklin to cut Kyle's painting out of the frame?"

"It was cut out?" Loi tilted her head. "I guess that's faster than opening the back of the frame, but you'd have to be careful because box cutters are sharp. Can I come along?" asked Loi. "Maybe I can help."

"That would be great," Connor said.

"Come on!" I started for the door. "Let's find our friends and see if they learned anything!"

We found our group.

"Mr. Lee had to move his car," said Kate. "He saw Franklin and Loi in the main hall when he was leaving."

My stomach went squiggly. That meant Franklin was near Kyle's painting when it was stolen.

"Don't worry, Lark," said Sophie. "Mr. Lee said he forgot his keys, so he turned around. That's when he saw Loi leaving Exhibit Hall A. Mr. Lee said he saw Franklin come out a couple of seconds after Loi."

"That means Franklin didn't have time to steal Kyle's canvas," said Loi.

"It's more than that," said Connor. "The canvas was already in Franklin's bag by then. It had already been stolen."

"This is amazing!" Kate hugged Franklin. "We can prove you didn't steal Kyle's work! You're back in the show!"

Our friends cheered, but for Connor and me, there was no cheering. We'd proven that Franklin didn't have time to cut out the canvas, stick it in his bag and run to us. That was one mystery solved, but a bigger mystery remained. Who had framed Franklin, and why had they done it?

Chapter Seven

When I told my friends my thoughts, they stopped cheering.

"That mystery is easily solved," said Sophie. "There's only one person who dislikes Franklin enough to do something like that."

"Kyle," said Connor. "It's time for him to answer some questions."

We found Kyle in the cafeteria, eating cheese and apples. "Did you come to apologize?" Kyle asked Franklin.

"More like *you* should apologize!" said Sophie.

Kate glowered and nodded. "We proved that Franklin didn't have time to steal your artwork," she said and then told him what we'd discovered.

"Some evidence," said Kyle. "You're Franklin's friends. You guys would say anything."

"But Mr. Lee wouldn't lie," I said. "And he backs up what everyone else is saying."

"Fine," Kyle muttered.

"I bet you framed Franklin," said Kate. "Everyone knows you don't like him."

I nodded. "You have a good motive for getting Franklin in trouble."

Kyle snorted. "This event is a big deal. Do you really think I dislike Franklin so much that I'd miss a chance to have my work on display and maybe even sold?"

Connor and I looked at each other. Kyle had a point. He might have a motive to hurt Franklin, but he didn't have a motive to hurt himself.

"Fine," said Kate. "You didn't take the painting, either."

"Great," Kyle grumbled. "Case solved. So now everything works out for Franklin."

"No. It's only part of the case solved," I said. "Someone messed with your work, and that's not right. We want to find out who did it."

"You're not really going to help me," said Kyle. "We're not friends."

"That's true—we're not friends," Connor said. "Because you're mean to us, no matter how kind we are to you. But a detective's job is to find the truth, and we will, no matter who is our friend."

"Before we help him," said Franklin, "there's something Kyle should say to me."

Kyle sighed. "You didn't do it."

"That's not good enough," said Franklin. "You almost got me kicked out of the show, and you're always mean to me. I don't deserve any of that."

Kyle ~~scowkled~~ ~~skowhold~~ scowled. "Fine. I'm sorry, okay? I'm sorry." He hopped off his chair. "I'm going to tell Mx. Tradewell that it wasn't you and make sure they don't kick you out of the show." He ran off.

Franklin sighed. "Sometimes it's really hard to remember to be patient with him."

Connor put his hand on Franklin's shoulder. "You did really good," he said.

Franklin smiled. Then he smiled bigger when Mx. Tradewell and Kyle came into the cafeteria.

"I'm so happy," said Mx. Tradewell. "I knew you couldn't have done it, Franklin!"

"But who did do it?" asked Kyle. "Who took my painting?"

That was a good question. "We're going to find the answer," I said.

"While you do that," said Mx. Tradewell, "Kyle, do you want to come with me? We have some unused frames in one of the storage areas. There should be one that'll fit your canvas."

Crickets! In solving the mystery of Kyle's canvas, we'd forgotten about the missing frame. "We should look for Kyle's frame," I said. "It might have a clue to the thief."

"You'll need my help," said Kyle. "I'm the one who knows what it looks like."

Mx. Tradewell checked their watch. "Okay. Kyle, meet me back here in ten minutes. If you haven't found your frame by then, we'll get a replacement one."

"We need to separate to look for it," I said. "Or else we won't have enough time."

"What does it look like?" asked Connor.

"It's a rectangle," said Kyle, "and it's made out of wood and stained dark brown." He shrugged. "It's simple, but it went really well with my painting, and I like it. A lot."

Once again our group split up. Kate, Franklin and Sophie went in one group to check the garbage cans. Loi and Kyle went to search the hallways and empty rooms. Connor and I went outside.

We searched around the building. We looked by trees and in bushes. Nothing. Connor and I split up and searched again. When I was done, I waited for him at the front of the gallery, but I kept my back to the glass. I didn't like seeing myself in the reflection. I looked extra grumpy because something felt off about the case, and I couldn't figure out what it was.

"Hey, Lark." Monty came outside, carrying a box of recyclables. "You look sad."

"I am," I said. "We figured out that Franklin didn't steal Kyle's painting."

"That sounds like great news," said Monty.

"But someone framed our friend," I said. "And I want to know who it was."

"That's terrible! I would be sad too." Monty set down his box. "Maybe I can help." He came over, sat down and folded his arms. "Go ahead," he said. "I'm listening."

I told him the whole story, finishing with "Plus, his frame is missing too."

Monty frowned. "I can see stealing Kyle's painting. It was amazing. But a missing frame? That's big and hard to hide. You can get a frame anywhere, but an original painting? Now *that's* valuable." He sighed. "I'm sorry, Lark, I'm not much help." He picked up his box. "But I'll keep thinking, and if I come up with any answers, I'll find you. Loi said there might be a mouse in the storage room of the main hall. I need to go and check."

I waved as he walked away. Then I went to find Connor, hoping he'd found the frame.

Chapter Eight

When I found Connor, his face was as sad as mine. "No luck?" I asked.

He shook his head, and we went to find our friends. They hadn't had any luck either.

"This is the pits," said Sophie.

"Wait a second." Connor thought for a moment. "We looked in the hallways, empty rooms, garbage cans and outside. Those are all logical places to look. What's an illogical place to hide a frame?"

"I know!" I said. "In a storage room with all the other frames!"

We rushed to find Mx. Tradewell and told them what we thought. They opened the storage room. "Kyle, do you see your frame?"

Kyle looked around carefully. "No," he said after he'd searched. "It's not here."

"Wait a second," said Loi. "What about the scuttling sounds we heard in the storage room in the main hall? I thought it was a mouse, but maybe I was wrong."

We checked, but there was no frame. We left the room. Mx. Tradewell locked the door, then went back to check on the exhibit.

Something kept ~~prikling prickelling~~ prickling my brain. I had an idea, but I wasn't sure if it was right. Good thing I had Connor and my friends with me. "Remember we were talking

65

about red herrings? What if this is another one?" I asked. "What if the person who took Kyle's artwork really wanted the frame, not the painting?"

Connor nodded. "I was wondering the same thing. I'm not sure if the person was purposely

trying to frame Franklin. Think about it. Franklin was the last person to leave, which means his bag was the only one left in the locker room."

"Exactly," I said. "The thief needed a spot to hide Kyle's painting. Franklin's bag just happened to be there."

"They wanted my frame?" said Kyle. "But I got it at Mrs. Robinson's garage sale. It was only twenty-five cents. It's not valuable."

"Maybe someone liked it too, and they wanted it, but Kyle got it first," Connor said. "Then that person saw the frame in the Exhibit Hall A and decided to take it. We should find Mrs. Robinson and see if she has any information for us."

We hurried to find Mrs. Robinson. She was looking at the pointillism paintings, and she smiled when she saw us.

"Hello," I said. "Did you sell a frame to Kyle?"

"Oh, yes," she said. "A couple of weeks ago. Why?"

We told her what had happened.

"Oh!" Her face got growly. "That's horrible. To steal a child's work and their property, and then to blame another child! I'm so angry, I can't even think of a word to describe how terrible that is."

I could think of a word. Almost. It started with a *d* or an *a*, and it meant to be truly horrible, terrible, despicable. It was a good word. "We can think of the word later," I said. "Right now, do you remember if anyone else wanted to buy the frame?"

"No," she said. "That thing sat there all day. It's why I let Kyle have it for twenty-five cents. I just wanted to get rid of it."

"Are you sure no one else wanted it?" I asked.

"No one," she said.

"See?" said Kyle. "I told you it wasn't valuable. Someone stole my artwork and took the frame because they knew they would look good together."

"That doesn't make sense," said Franklin, "because we have your painting but not the frame."

Kyle's face went blank. Then it went pouty. "I hate all of this," he said. "That frame was perfect for my painting. Now my painting has been cut, and I have to use a different frame." He blinked hard. "This was my chance to prove I was the best at something. Everyone in my family is the best at something," he said. "My dad is the best at cooking. My mom won an award at work for her building designs. Even my little brother has won—he was named most valuable player on his soccer team."

"I don't understand," said Kate. "You're good at so many things."

"But I'm not the best," said Kyle. He pointed at Franklin. "He's always beating me."

"Wait a second!" said Franklin. "Is that why you're so mean to me?"

"Why do you have to be so good at everything?" Kyle swiped his eyes. "Why can't you let me win sometimes?"

"I'm not going to stop trying my hardest just so you feel better," said Franklin.

Kyle sniffed again, then nodded. "I really am sorry."

"Thank you," said Franklin. "I accept your apology."

Crickets. We had our motive for Kyle being so mean to Franklin, but we still didn't know why the culprit had taken Kyle's frame.

"Kids?" Mx. Tradewell came up to us. "The show's going to start in fifteen minutes. Do you know what happened to Kyle's frame?"

"No," said Connor. "We don't."

"This is terrible," said Kate. "We still haven't solved this!"

Loi puffed out a frustrated breath. "I thought helping would be fun and easy, but it's so much harder than I thought!"

"You tried your best," said Mx. Tradewell. "Kyle, why don't you come with me and we'll find a new frame for you?"

While Kyle and Mx. Tradewell went to the storage room, the rest of our friends went to the cafeteria for a snack.

"Come on," Connor said with a sigh. "We'd better go and meet Mom, Dad and Halmoni."

I couldn't believe Connor and I had a case we couldn't solve. Today had really become my worstest day ever. I followed my brother out of the gallery and into the sunshine to find our family.

Chapter Nine

"Cool! It's our surprise!" shouted Connor.

I'd forgotten that Mom and Dad had promised us a surprise that morning, and it was the best surprise ever! "Babu! How are you here? We just talked to you in Kenya."

"We played a trick," said Babu. "I pretended to be in Kenya, but really I was at the airport, waiting for your mom and dad to pick me up."

I ran and jumped into his arms. "And now you're here!"

He laughed and hugged me tight. Then he hugged Connor tight. "Our research project ended early, and I thought it would be great fun to surprise you!"

"It *is* great fun!" I said. "I want to hear about the elephants."

"Me too," said Connor. "Did you pick a name for the baby?"

"I emailed the team your name suggestion, and they loved it!" said Babu. "So the calf's name is Halley."

"Speaking of fun," said Dad, "did you have fun looking at Franklin's work?"

His question reminded me of everything that had happened, and I stopped smiling. We sat with our family at a picnic table outside the gallery, and Connor and I told them everything.

"My goodness," said Halmoni after we'd finished. "I don't know how I feel. It sounds like Kyle is mending his relationship with Franklin, and I'm happy about that. But I don't know if I'm happy that it took the theft of his work to do it. Poor Kyle. I'm sure he worked hard on his art."

Mom nodded. "I'm so proud of the two of you, not just for helping Franklin, but for helping Kyle too. It's easy to step in for our friends. It's a lot harder to do it with people who test our patience."

Dad kissed the tops of our heads. "You two are amazing."

"I don't feel amazing," Connor said. "I feel grumpy that we didn't solve the case."

"Come with me," said Babu. He took us to the glass walls of the gallery. Babu knelt down and put his arms around us. "Do you see what I see?" he asked. "I see two people who spent their summer helping those around them. I see two of the kindest, smartest people I know." He pulled us closer. "There's still time before the show begins, so keep thinking. But even if you don't solve this case, you're still the smartest, kindest people I know."

"Thanks, Babu," said Connor.

"I hope you're as proud of yourselves as I am," he said.

I looked at our reflection. We had had a lot of fun this summer helping out our friends. Babu and Mx. Tradewell were right. We'd tried our hardest, and we should be proud of ourselves.

"I'm proud of us," said Connor. "I'm—Lark!"

"Crickets!" I yelled at the same time and looked at Connor.

"We know who did it!" we shouted.

"Mx. Tradewell! Mx. Tradewell!" I called out to the gallery owner as Connor and I rushed inside, our family right behind us.

Mx. Tradewell was in the main hall. They grinned. "You look like you have an answer to our mystery."

"We do," I said. "It was Monty."

Mx. Tradewell's mouth dropped open. "Monty?"

"Did someone call me?" Monty came up to us as our friends gathered around.

"Monty," I said, "you need to give Kyle back his frame."

Monty's eyebrows went up. "You think I did this?"

"We *know* you did this," said Connor.

Monty shook his head sadly. "I didn't, and you can't prove I did. What a terrible thing to accuse me of."

"This case was all about red herrings," I said. "There was wet paint on the easel, but none of the other paintings had wet paint. There were scuttling sounds in the main hall's storage room, but the room was empty."

"At first we thought the mystery was about the painting, but it was really about the missing frame," said Connor.

"So?" said Monty. "How does that make me the culprit?"

"Because you are the biggest red herring of all," I said. "You are a security guard who is doing all kinds of things that a security guard doesn't do. You were watering plants and taking out the recycling."

"That's because everyone was busy with the event," Monty said, his voice hard. "I told you, I was helping out."

"Exactly," said Connor. "You said Ms. Jensen waved at you and sprayed herself with water. But the gallery walls are reflective glass. With the sun shining, she couldn't have seen you inside. She never waved. You were outside so no one would think it was you who stole Kyle's painting and frame."

"Then you said that Loi told you about the mouse," I added. "But Loi never got a chance to talk to you. The only reason you knew about it is because you were in the storage room. You made the scuttling sounds that Loi and Franklin heard."

"Monty," Mx. Tradewell said quietly, "is there something you want to say?"

A clue flashed in my brain. "Ask him to show us his hands," I said. "Every time I saw him today, his hands were hidden by gloves or a box or were in his pockets."

"Loi said box cutters are sharp," said Connor. "He might have cut himself."

Monty hid his hands behind his back.

"But that frame was only twenty-five cents," said Kyle. "It's not valuable."

"Shows what you know!" Monty burst out. "It's a frame from the early twentieth century. It's worth hundreds of dollars!"

Kyle's eyes went wide. "But it only cost me twenty-five cents."

"Because you don't know as much about art as I do," said Monty. "I've worked in this gallery for years. I know all about paintings—and their frames. When I saw yours, I knew how valuable it was, and I had to have it."

"You stole from a child," Babu said, disgusted.

"And you let another child be blamed for it." added Halmoni with a serious face.

"But I didn't take his artwork," Monty said desperately. "That should count for something!"

He held up his hands. Two of his fingers were covered in bandages.

"You can talk to the police officers about that," said Mx. Tradewell. "Where is the frame?"

A final clue flashed in my brain. "He took a box of recycling outside. I bet it's hidden in there."

"You're coming with me to the office so we can call Officer Duong. Let's go." Mx. Tradewell turned to Connor and me. "That was amazing detective work. While I take care of this matter, how would the two of you like to be the ones who open the show?"

"That would be awesome," said Connor. "But this was all of us. Can we and all our friends start the show?"

"Of course," said Mx. Tradewell. They left with Monty.

"That was amazing!" Babu gave us a high five. "Now quick, open the show!"

We started for the stage. I turned back when Kyle didn't move. "Come on!" I said. "You're part of our group!"

"Are you sure?" he asked. "I haven't been a friend to any of you."

"But you helped," said Connor. "And that counts."

"And you're going to be a friend now, right?" said Franklin. "No more being mean to anyone."

Kyle took a breath. "I'll try my best."

I joined my friends onstage. We'd solved a mystery full of red herrings, maybe found a new friend, and Babu was home for a visit. Today— and this summer—had been the bestest day and summer ever!

THE WORDS LARK LOVES

CHAPTER TWO:

"You mean like..." I tried to think of the word. It was a good one, and it started with a c or an s, and it meant to be sneaky and destroy people's stuff.

The awesome word Lark was thinking of is *sabotage*, which means to purposely damage or destroy someone else's property.

CHAPTER EIGHT:

I could think of a word. Almost. It started with a d or an a, and it meant to be truly horrible, terrible, despicable.

The word Lark was thinking of is *dastardly*, which means everything Lark said and more. It describes behavior that's not just horrible, terrible and despicable, but also sneaky, cowardly and cruel.

THE STUFF LARK *ALMOST* GOT RIGHT

CHAPTER TWO:

"Your parents and I will meet you for the show. We'll be there with bells on!"

Lark and Connor didn't quite understand what Halmoni meant by this phrase. To "be there with bells on" means to be excited to attend an event. Halmoni meant she was thrilled to see the show.

CHAPTER FIVE:

"A penny for your thoughts," Mx. Tradewell said
to me.

Lark thought Mx. Tradewell was offering her
money to share her thoughts. But "a penny for
your thoughts" is another way to ask, "What are
you thinking?" or "What's on your mind?"

DON'T MISS THE REST OF THE
LARK BA
DETECTIVE SERIES

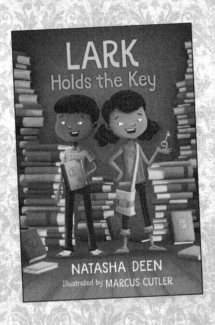

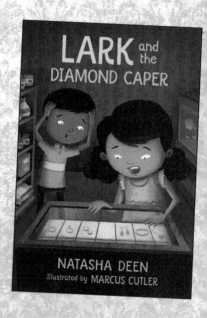

"A problem-solving adventure
led by a lovable character."
—*SCHOOL LIBRARY JOURNAL*

"Lark's sparkly presence on the chapter-book shelves will be welcomed by many."
—*KIRKUS REVIEWS*

NATASHA DEEN loves stories: exciting ones, scary ones and, especially, funny ones! As a kid of two countries (Guyana and Canada), she feels especially lucky because she gets a double dose of stories. Natasha is the author of many books, including the Lark Ba Detective series in the Orca Echoes line, *Thicker Than Water* in the Orca Soundings line and *In the Key of Nira Ghani*, which won the Amy Mathers Teen Book Award and was nominated for the Red Maple Award. Natasha lives in Edmonton.